William Steig
Potch & Polly
with pictures by
Jon Agee
Farrar
Straus
Giroux
New York

WHEN POTCH WAS BORN, there was an angel with a clown's face hovering over the bed. So Potch came into the world laughing.

HA
HA
HA

As a child, he so relished the gift of life that it was almost impossible for his mother or the servants to get him to go to sleep. He'd pummel the pillows, twist, shout, stretch, and start making speeches in a language only he understood.

Even as a grownup, Potch turned off the lights reluctantly, and always woke up happy to be who and where he was.

Then one fateful morning, Gammon, his butler, brought him an invitation to attend, that very night, a glorious masquerade ball. "Yippee!" cried Potch. "I'll be a skeleton—no clothes, just bones."

"A hippopotamus would be more appropriate," said Gammon.

"Very funny," said Potch.

Potch spent all day climbing in and out of his many costumes. "Ta de da doodle da," he finally said. "I shall be Harlequin himself."

LADIE AND
GENT MEN!

Potch was having a ball at the ball when two brightly colored parrots flew in. “Ladies and gentlemen,” they squawked, “please welcome the preternatural Polly Pumpernickel!” And Potch, for the first time, saw her. He was so smitten, he did a double backflip.

A moment later the two were dancing.

SUGAR

Polly Pumpernickel, to tell the truth, was no beauty. But to Potch, who was no beauty himself, she was a sugar bowl. It dawned on him that love had been missing from his life, the same love that makes the world go round and can turn pigs into ponies.

What an evening! The crowd stared as the pair continued to prance and pirouette, to weave and whirl. Polly thought Potch might be the daffy darling of her daily dreams, the one missing piece of her pie.

But then Potch flung Polly up in the air and . . .

Missed catching her!

"YOU DUMB DODO!" she screamed.

Potch moped the whole way home. "I really bumbled things up," he sighed.

The next morning, Potch tugged on a tasseled rope, and his whole staff came tumbling in. Together they devised a plan for him to win the heart of Polly.

The town clock was striking one when a large box was delivered to Polly's house.

Polly hesitated, trying to guess what it could be—
a love seat? a statue? She opened the lid. Empty!
Then out popped Potch, from a secret trapdoor.

Polly stared as Potch raised a wand commanding
attention. He tapped on the box twice and behold:

1
THREE EGGS

2
JUGGLING

3
SPLAT!

4
SHOW'S OVER!

BWAH!

Potch was unfazed by this flop. The following day he rode up to Polly's window on a circus elephant, and announced his arrival with a trumpet.

Unfortunately, the path he took was through her precious garden of rare roses.

Polly was furious. "You overgrown oaf," she hollered, and flung her dictionary at him.

BANG

But Potch still had plenty of pep. And purpose. That evening, he encircled Polly's house with Roman candles. The fireworks that followed lit up the sky.

All except one.

Polly's eyes glowed green with rage.

At sunup she approached Potch's house, determined to put an end to his pestering. She saw him ensconced in his hammock, talking to an angel with a big red nose.

"Why are you hanging there like a piece of macaroni?" asked the angel.

"Simple," said Potch. "I'm in love with Polly Pumpernickel."

HEY!

"Potch," said his angel, "Polly Pumpernickel will never understand your kind of love. Pin a medal on her and send her packing."

He flapped his wings and flew away, smiling as he passed over the spot where he knew Polly was hiding.

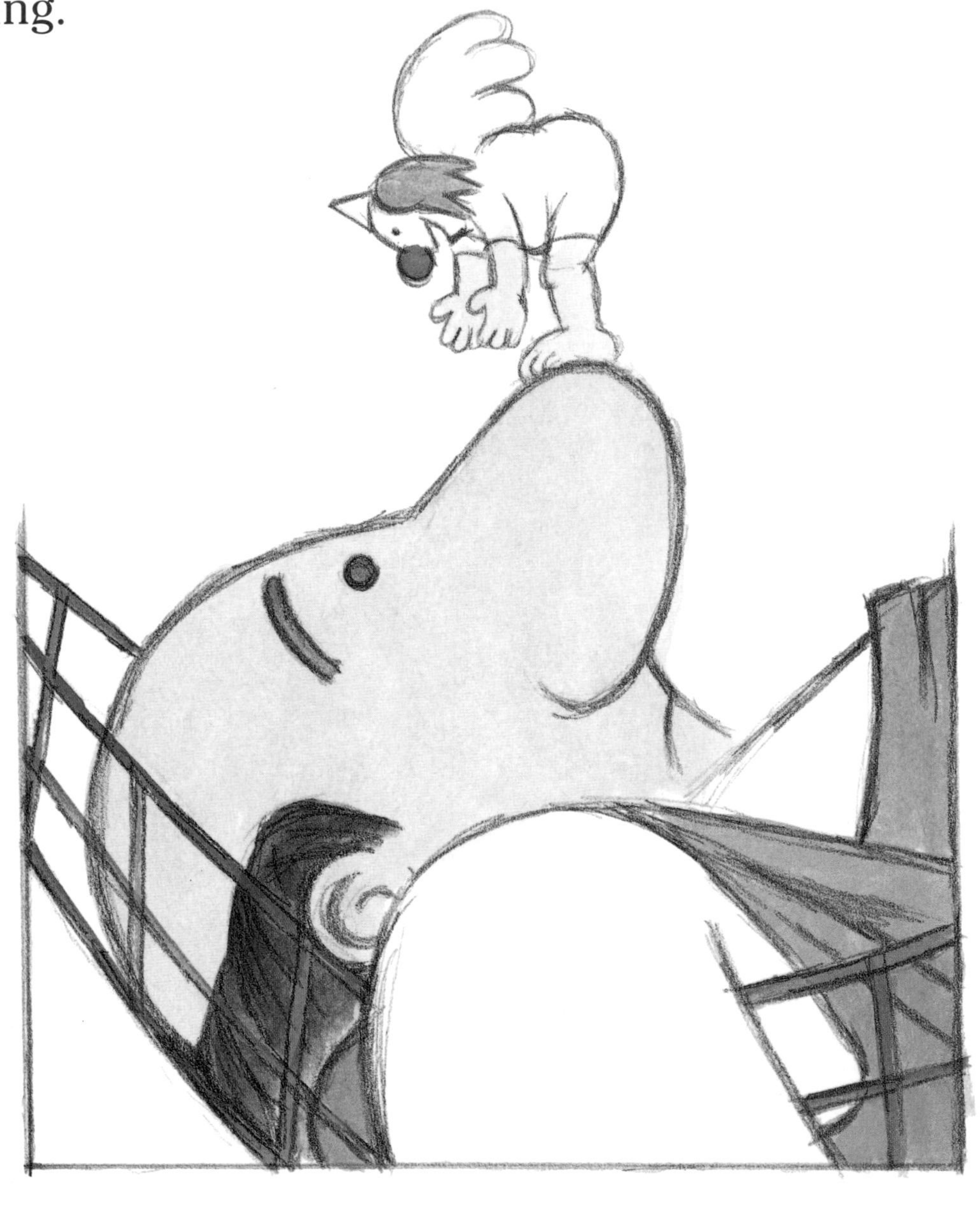

"Send me packing?" Polly muttered. "Hmm." She stole out of the bushes and hurried home.

GLU
NAILS

Polly got busy.

That night, the town clock was striking eight when a large box was delivered to Potch's house.

"Shall I open it?" Gammon asked.

"Open, shmopen," said Potch, "what do I care?"

Gammon lifted the lid. Empty!

HOWDEE DOODLE-DOO!

Then out popped Polly, from a secret trapdoor.

"Polly?" said Potch.

"It's me," said she.

They both laughed, and somewhere music started playing. A moment later they were dancing.

For Mo and Easy —W.S.   For Bill —J.A.

 Distributed in Canada by Douglas & McIntyre Ltd.
Color separations by Hong Kong Scanner Arts
Printed and bound in the United States by Berryville Graphics
Designed by Jennifer Crilly
First edition, 2002

Library of Congress Cataloging-in-Publication Data
Steig, William, date.
Potch & Polly / William Steig ; pictures by Jon Agee.— 1st ed.
p. cm.
Summary: Lively Potch pursues the girl of his dreams,
the darling Polly Pumpernickel.
ISBN 0-374-36090-1
[1. Love—Fiction. 2. Courtship—Fiction.]
I. Title: Potch and Polly. II. Agee, Jon, ill. III. Title.
PZ7.S8177 Po 2002
[E]—dc21
00-29544